EGMONT
We bring stories to life

First Published in Great Britain 2017
by Egmont UK Limited, The Yellow Building,
1 Nicholas Road, London W11 4AN

Written by Katrina Pallant
Designed by Maddox Philpot
Crafts by Kate Rhodes
Illustrations by Chris Chatterton

© & ™ 2017 Lucasfilm Ltd.

ISBN 978 1 4052 7997 0
62262/1
Printed in China

For more great *Star Wars* books, visit www.egmont.co.uk/starwars

Stay safe online. Any website addresses listed in this book are correct at the
time of going to print. However, Egmont is not responsible for content hosted by
third parties. Please be aware that online content can be subject to change and
we sites can contain content that is unsuitable for children. We advise that all
children are supervised when using the internet.

CONTENTS

CRAFT RULES

Over the next few pages you will learn how to make some awesome *Star Wars* crafts, so here are a few rules to help keep you safe and having fun!

- Always ask a parent/guardian before beginning a new craft.
- Cover any surfaces with newspaper when painting or gluing.
- For younglings, make sure you have a grown-up with you when cutting with sharp scissors. You may also need their help for the trickier steps.
- Make sure you have permission from your parent/guardian to use any materials found around the house.
- Do not try to use an iron by yourself, always ask a grown-up to assist you.

CHEWBACCA HAND PUPPET

MATERIALS

- A large piece of paper and a pen or pencil
- Long-pile brown fur fabric
- Pins and a needle
- Scissors
- Brown thread
- Brown felt for belt & hands
- Cream felt for teeth
- Pale pink felt for gums
- Darker pink felt for inner mouth
- PVA glue
- Tin foil
- Newspaper
- Foam sponge
- Two large flat white buttons
- Two small blue buttons
- A black marker pen
- Silver paper
- Black paint
- Paintbrush
- A small piece of folded card (for the mouth)
- Double-sided tape

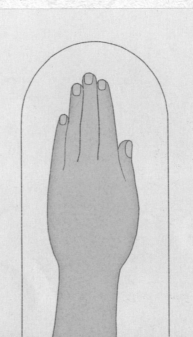

1 On a large piece of paper draw around your hand, with your fingers together, leaving approximately 30mm all around. Fold your paper in half and draw an arm on one side. Make the arm fairly wide, especially where it joins the body. You will need to push the arm up inside itself so that you can turn your Wookiee inside out. Cut out your pattern.

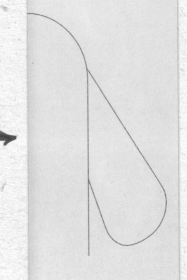

2

Unfold your pattern and lay it on the reverse side of your fur fabric. Draw around it and cut it out. Repeat this step so that you have two identical pieces.

3

Pin your fabric with the fur side together facing inwards, and sew around the edge. Leave the base of the body open. Carefully make a small snip up to the stitching under the arms.

4

Cut a straight line between the top of the arms for Chewbacca's mouth. Carefully cut through one layer of fabric only, leaving about 40mm of fabric at either side uncut.

5

Gently push the body fabric inside out starting with the arms.

6

Fold a piece of card in half and cut out a semicircle to fit inside Chewbacca's mouth. Cover the card in double-sided tape.

7

Using this card as a guide, cut out a piece of dark pink felt for inside Chewbacca's mouth and a ring of light pink felt for his gums.

9 For the eyes, take two flat white buttons and draw on eyelids using a marker pen. Stick a smaller blue button in the middle of each one for the pupil. Sew in place.

10 Mould a nose out of tin foil and then cover in papier mâché (use PVA thinned with water and strips of newspaper). Allow drying time before painting black. When the paint has dried, glue in to place.

8

Stick the card inside Chewbacca's mouth and add the two pieces of felt on top. Cut out teeth from the cream felt and stick around the gums.

11

Cut a piece of foam in a semicircle and glue right up inside Chewbacca's head (above his mouth) to give a bit more shape.

12 Cut two strips (approximately 4x20cm) from brown felt to make the bandolier. Glue the ends together to make a loop.

15 Finally, cut out two hands from brown felt and stick in place at the end of Chewbacca's arms.

13 Cut 6 small pieces of foam sponge (approximately 5x3x1cm) and cover with silver paper. Glue these an even distance apart on one side of the bandolier.

14 Cut a second strip of felt 2cm wide and glue on and over the sponge squares. Glue or sew the bandolier in place over his shoulder so that it goes round and across the front of his body.

FINGER PUPPETS

MATERIALS

- Coloured felt
- Pen/pencil and paper
- Scissors
- Coloured thread and a needle
- Googly eyes
- PVA glue

1 Draw around your finger onto paper leaving a 10mm margin, and cut out.

2 To make Yoda: Tracing around your paper template, cut two pieces of light brown felt and one piece of dark brown.

3 Place the dark brown felt on top of one piece of light brown felt and carefully sew around the outside edge, leaving the bottom open. This will form the basic shape of your finger puppet.

Take the second piece of light brown felt and cut an arch on either side. Glue the arch-shaped pieces to the front of the puppet for Yoda's robe.

4

Draw Yoda's head on a piece of paper and cut out. Tracing around your template cut two pieces from the green felt.

7

Glue Yoda's head to the top of the body and glue the second head shape to the reverse.

To finish, glue Yoda's lightsaber in place and add a hand to hold it.

5 Taking one of the green heads, sew Yoda's frown lines, nose and mouth in darker green thread. To make a solid line, first sew one way and then sew back along the same line between the gaps.

TRY DIFFERENT COLOURS AND SHAPES TO CREATE OTHER FAVOURITE CHARACTERS!

6 Add googly eyes, and from darker green felt cut and glue inner ears in place.

STORMTROOPER HELMET

MATERIALS

- A balloon
- Papier mâché – using 1 part PVA to 2 parts water
- Old newspaper
- PVA glue
- Tape
- A bowl
- Scissors
- Plain white card
- Brown corrugated card
- Cardboard tubes
- Two small bottle tops
- Two large bottle tops/lids
- White paint
- Black paint
- A paintbrush

MIX 1 PART PVA WITH 2 PARTS PAINT. THIS WILL HELP THE PAINT STICK TO ANY PLASTIC AREAS, LIKE THE BOTTLE TOPS. YOUR MASK WILL NEED SEVERAL COATS OF PAINT TO COVER THE NEWSPAPER. ALLOW DRYING TIME BETWEEN EACH COAT.

1

Blow up a balloon so that the circumference at the widest part is about 5cm larger than your head, measuring around your head at eyebrow level. Using little bits of torn-up newspaper, papier mâché over the top of the balloon, following the shape of a hairline, so slightly higher at the front than the back. Build up several layers of papier mâché and let this dry.

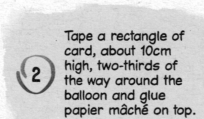

2 Tape a rectangle of card, about 10cm high, two-thirds of the way around the balloon and glue papier mâché on top.

3 Cut a piece of tube at an angle to form the nose area of the mask. Cut out a section three quarters of the way along the tube and tape into place above the cut out with card.
Tip – sit your balloon in a bowl to work on your mask!

13

Cut sections of tube
and stick around the
base of the mask.
The two either side
of the nose should
be slightly angled.
Stuff scrunched up
newspaper inside the
tubes at the joins.

Papier mâché over the
tubes and any joins in your
mask to hold in place.

To make the chin, cut
an arch shape from
corrugated card. Peel
off the first layer
to reveal the bumpy
part in the middle and
stick in place. Cut two
v-shaped pieces of
plain card to fit either
side of the cut-out
section in the nose to
make the mouth indent.

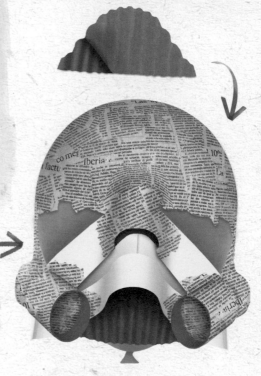

From corrugated card, cut
out two eye shapes and stick
in to place. Cut a thin strip
and stick above the eyes,
around the head from side to
side, but not around the back.

8

Papier mâché over your mask covering any joins and just leave the chin as bumpy corrugated card. Carefully pop your balloon and make sure there are no broken pieces of balloon left behind. Tidy up any rough areas on the inside of your mask.

9

Stick a large bottle top/lid on either side of the mask (where the ears would be) and a small bottle top inside the tubes at the front. Add papier mâché to any joins and let the glue dry.

10

Now paint your mask to finish! Start by painting the whole mask white.

Then add the final details in black.

X-WING MODEL

MATERIALS

- Long tube (like the roll from inside wrapping paper)
- Tape
- Thick card for the wings and engines
- Thinner card for the cockpit
- Pen tops – various shapes & sizes
- Bottle lids that fit the width of the tube
- 4 pen middles
- Newspaper
- PVA glue
- Various paints – white, black, red, yellow, pale grey/green
- Paintbrush & saucer for mixing
- Sponge

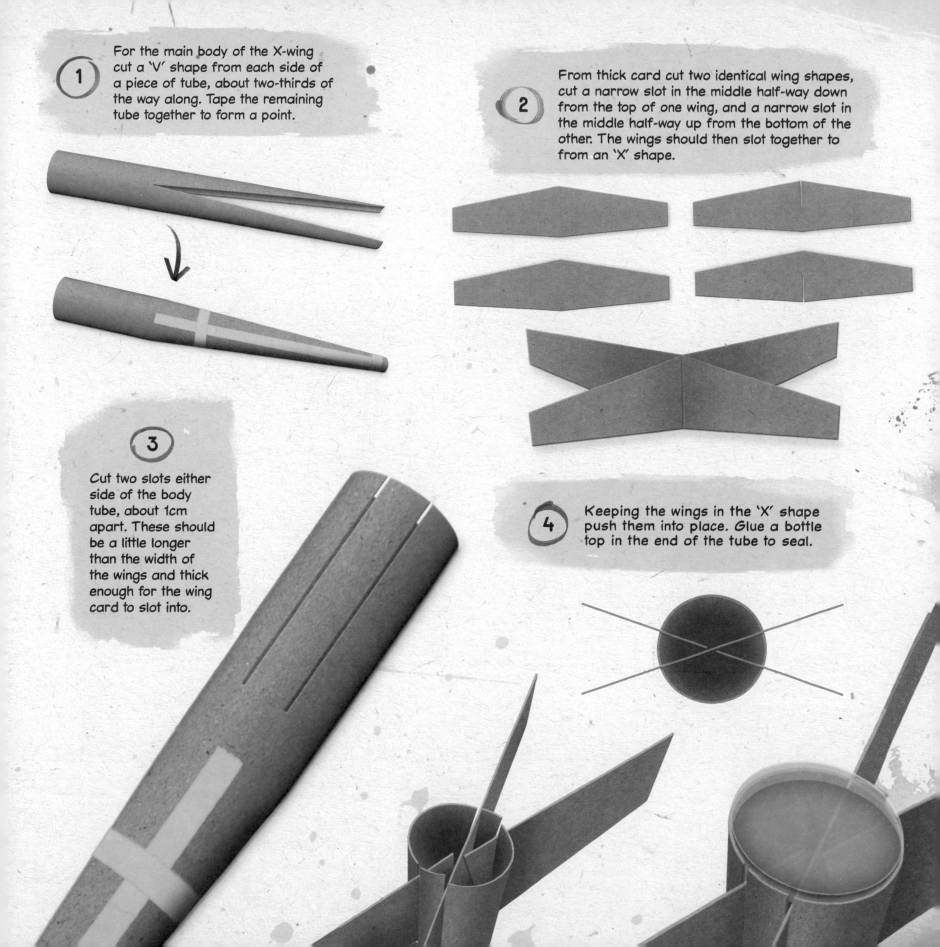

1 For the main body of the X-wing cut a 'V' shape from each side of a piece of tube, about two-thirds of the way along. Tape the remaining tube together to form a point.

2 From thick card cut two identical wing shapes, cut a narrow slot in the middle half-way down from the top of one wing, and a narrow slot in the middle half-way up from the bottom of the other. The wings should then slot together to from an 'X' shape.

3 Cut two slots either side of the body tube, about 1cm apart. These should be a little longer than the width of the wings and thick enough for the wing card to slot into.

4 Keeping the wings in the 'X' shape push them into place. Glue a bottle top in the end of the tube to seal.

5 Cut the shape shown below from card to form the cockpit. Make sure the middle section is as wide as your tube, and that the front section is longer than the back. Fold as shown and stick into place between the wings.

6 Push a large pen top (like a highlighter pen) to the end of the tube and papier mâché over the joins, along the tube and over the cockpit.

7 Cut four sections of tube and stick one to each wing near the cockpit. They should be positioned towards the front of the wing and be slightly shorter than the width. Then stick a felt pen top, centred, to the far end of each wing. Papier mâché over any joins.

8 Push a bottle top in the end of each tube, and papier mâché in place. Glue a thin piece of card across the width of each top to make the engines.

9 Paint your model white and leave to dry.

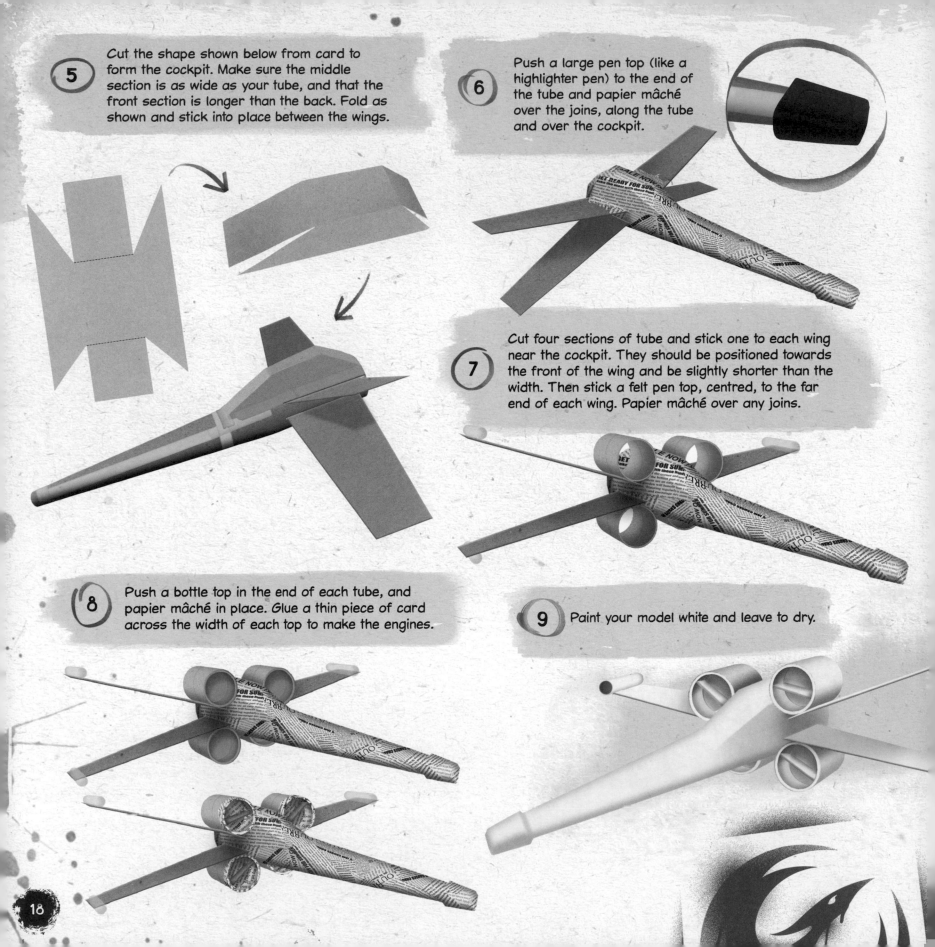

10 Then add details in red, yellow and black.

11 Take four ballpoint pens and remove the inkwells. Dip the ends in glue to seal and let them dry. Then paint with a mix of PVA and white paint.

12 Glue one inside each pen top facing forwards.

13 Glue another pen top inside the back of each tube and paint with a mix of PVA and white paint.

14 To finish, dip a sponge in grey and pale green paint to add a distressed, slightly old and battered feel.

YODA DECODER

MATERIALS

- Paper or card
- Letters cut from a newspaper (or just use a pen!)
- Aurebesh letters from the art pad
- Sticky tape
- 2 split pins (one for each decoder – your friend will need one too!)
- A compass
- A ruler
- A protractor would be useful although not essential.

1

Using a compass, draw a circle on a piece of card and cut out.

2

Lightly draw a circle about 15mm from the outside edge to use as a guide. Then, using the compass point in the centre, draw a straight line across the middle (again do this lightly as it will be a guide for placing the letters).

3 The circle needs to be divided into 26 segments, so each segment will be approximately 14 degrees. A protractor is good for this, but if you don't have one divide each quarter into 6 and a half using a ruler.

4 Cut out the letters of the *Star Wars* alphabet from your art pad and arrange around the circle. Glue into place.

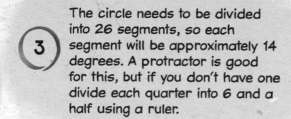

5 Cut a smaller circle and cut out a window slightly larger than the size of a letter. This will reveal your code when you turn the wheel.

Attach to the larger circle with a split pin.

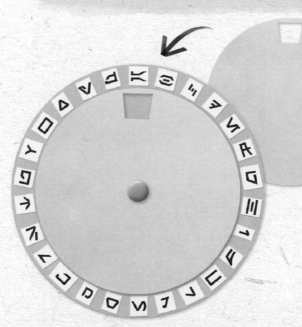

6 As you turn the wheel write the English letter for your code in the window under the corresponding Aurebesh letter around the outside edge.

GRAB A FRIEND AND SEND SECRET MESSAGES TO EACH OTHER THAT ONLY YOU CAN DECODE!

DARTH MAUL T-SHIRT

MATERIALS

- Template of Darth Maul
- Tracing paper
- Card
- Pencil
- Scissors
- Double-sided tape
- A plain black T-shirt
- Old newspaper
- Red, black and yellow fabric paint
- An old toothbrush for the spatter effect on the red T-shirt

1

Trace a picture of Darth Maul using the template on the next page. Cut out the eyes and all the sections that you would like to appear red to make your stencil.

2

This is a messy make so start by covering your work surface in newspaper. Lay your plain black T-shirt flat and put some newspaper inside to stop any paint seeping through to the reverse.

3 Stick little strips of double-sided tape on the reverse of your stencil and stick in place on the front of your T-shirt.

4

Paint all the areas that show through your stencil red, except for the eyes. Once dry remove your stencil carefully and ask an adult to cover with a dry towel and iron to fix, following the instructions on the label.

Note: Painting on a black or dark T-shirt may require several layers of paint, so keep repeating these stages until you are happy with the colour. You can replace your stencil, or use your first layer of paint as a guide.

5

Fancy a red T-shirt instead? Cut out the areas that you would like to appear black, and paint. When the paint has dried remove the stencil and to finish paint the eyes.

6

To add a little definition to Darth Maul's face you could use an old toothbrush to flick paint around the edge. Do this with the stencil in place.

7

When the paint has dried remove the stencil and to finish paint the eyes.

As before remember to ask an adult to fix the paint with an iron.

BLACK T-SHIRT
STENCIL TEMPLATE

RED T-SHIRT
STENCIL TEMPLATE

LEARN
TO DRAW

YOU WILL NEED:

A SHARP PENCIL
YOU SHOULD WORK LIGHT AND FAST TO CREATE INITIAL SKETCHES

A BLACK FELT TIP
ONCE YOU HAVE CREATED A PENCIL SKETCH YOU ARE HAPPY WITH, MAKE IT BOLD WITH A FINE BLACK LINE

AN ERASER - TO REMOVE ANY
MISTAKES AND YOUR INITIAL PENCIL LINES

COLOURING PENCILS - WHEN YOU ARE
HAPPY WITH YOUR PICTURE BRING IT TO LIFE WITH A BIT OF COLOUR!

DOS AND DON'TS:

DO USE YOUR ERASER TO TIDY UP YOUR SKETCHES

DO WORK FROM THE INSIDE OUT

DO WORK LOOSE, FAST AND MESSY

DO PRACTISE

DON'T WORRY ABOUT BEING PERFECT

DON'T WORK TINY AND DARK

DON'T HUNCH TOO CLOSELY OVER YOUR DRAWINGS

THIS GRAND MASTER IS ONE OF THE MOST POWERFUL JEDI IN GALACTIC HISTORY. LEARN TO DRAW HIM, YOU WILL!

1

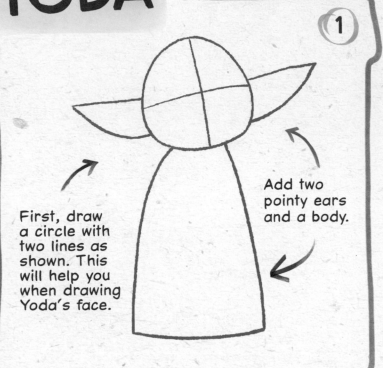

First, draw a circle with two lines as shown. This will help you when drawing Yoda's face.

Add two pointy ears and a body.

2

Add ovals in the shape of Yoda's arms, hands and toes.

Draw Yoda's eyes, nose and mouth using the lines as a guide.

3

Add details to Yoda's face and ears.

Draw Yoda's robe with long sleeves and add his stick.

4

Give Yoda some hair and wrinkles.

Add details to Yoda's robe.

Don't forget Yoda's finger and toenails.

Now rub out your rough lines and colour Yoda in!

FINAL

DO OR DO NOT, THERE IS NO TRY

FACT FILE

- UNKNOWN SPECIES

- GRAND MASTER OF THE JEDI COUNCIL

- INSTRUCTS LUKE SKYWALKER IN THE WAYS OF THE FORCE

- LIVES TO BE 900 YEARS OLD

- RENOWNED FOR HIS GREAT WISDOM

DARTH VADER

THE GREATEST *STAR WARS* VILLAIN IS DANGEROUS WITH A LIGHTSABER. DRAW HIS FAMOUS BLACK SUIT AND RED WEAPON.

1

Draw a stick figure with lightsaber at the ready!

2

Draw ovals for Vader's arms and legs and a long torso.

Add a glow around his lightsaber.

3

Draw Vader's famous helmet.

Add his cloak, and details to his suit.

4

Finish off the final details of his outfit.

Rub out any lines you don't need and colour in this Dark Lord of the Sith.

FINAL

THE FORCE IS STRONG WITH THIS ONE

FACT FILE

- ANAKIN SKYWALKER TURNS TO THE DARK SIDE TO BECOME DARTH VADER

- HAS TO WEAR A SPECIAL SUIT FOR LIFE SUPPORT

- FATHER OF LUKE SKYWALKER AND PRINCESS LEIA

- MENTORED BY DARTH SIDIOUS

R2-D2

A RESOURCEFUL DROID WHO IS READY FOR ANYTHING, R2-D2 IS A HERO OF THE REBELLION.

1

Start with a long dome shape for R2's body.

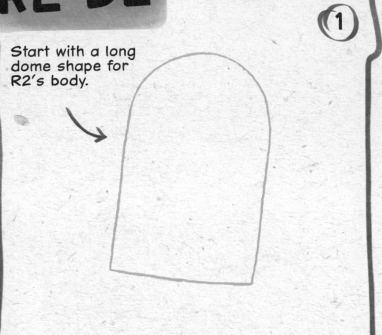

2

R2's legs are made up of four shapes.

Don't forget his bottom leg. This helps him whizz about!

3

Add detail to his legs and base.

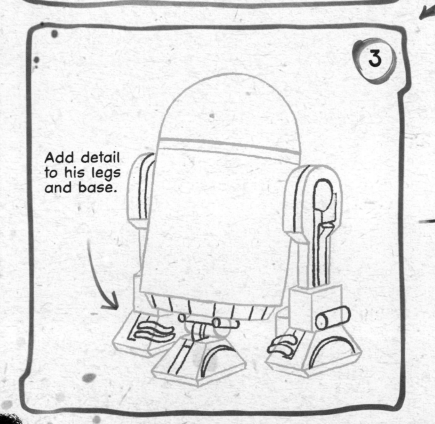

4

Finish R2 off with the detail on his face and body.

Rub out any lines you don't need and colour in this famous astromech.

FINAL

BLEEP
BLEEP
BLOOP

FACT FILE

- R2 SERIES ASTROMECH DROID

- DELIVERS THE DEATH STAR PLANS TO OBI-WAN KENOBI FOR PRINCESS LEIA

- FLIES WITH LUKE IN THE BATTLE OF YAVIN

- LONG-TIME COMPANION OF C-3PO

C-3PO

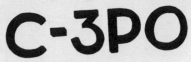

1

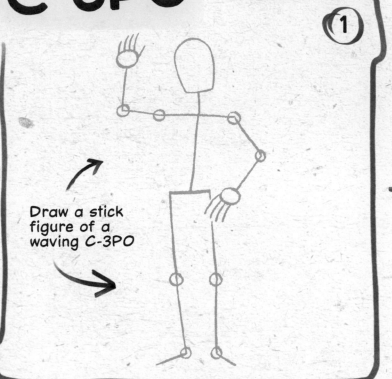

Draw a stick figure of a waving C-3PO

2

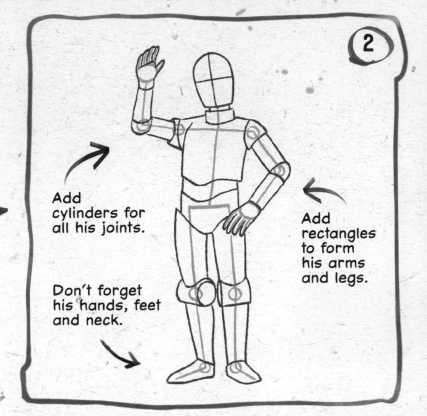

Add cylinders for all his joints.

Add rectangles to form his arms and legs.

Don't forget his hands, feet and neck.

3

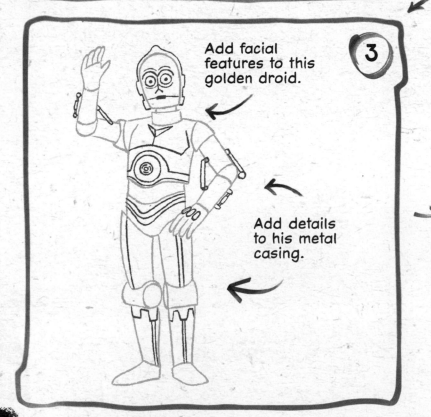

Add facial features to this golden droid.

Add details to his metal casing.

4

Finish C-3PO off with his wiring and final details.

Rub out any lines you don't need and colour C-3PO in.

HELLO, I'M C-3PO, HUMAN-CYBORG RELATIONS

FINAL

FACT FILE

- FLUENT IN OVER SEVEN MILLION FORMS OF COMMUNICATION

- BUILT BY ANAKIN SKYWALKER

- PROGRAMMED FOR ETIQUETTE

- TENDS TO PANIC WHEN PLACED IN DANGEROUS SITUATIONS

OBI-WAN

THIS LEGENDARY JEDI IS HIGHLY SKILLED IN THE WAYS OF THE FORCE. SUMMON YOUR SKILLS TO DRAW THIS WISE WARRIOR.

1

Add Obi-Wan's head and arms.

Start with a long shape that is circular at the bottom and flat at the top.

2

Add the details of Obi-Wan's Jedi robe as shown.

Don't forget his billowing sleeves and belt.

3

Add Obi-Wan's facial features.

Draw Obi-Wan's lightsaber – a civilised weapon.

4

Add the final details to Obi-Wan's robe.

Rub out any lines you don't need and colour in this Jedi Master.

THAT'S NO MOON

FINAL

FACT FILE

- MENTOR TO BOTH ANAKIN AND LUKE SKYWALKER

- DEFEATS SITH LORD DARTH MAUL DURING THE BATTLE OF NABOO

- DEFEATED BY DARTH VADER, HIS FORMER PADAWAN

LUKE

THIS FORMER TATOOINE FARMBOY RISES TO BE ONE OF THE GREATEST JEDI IN HISTORY, AND AN ACE X-WING PILOT TOO!

1

Start with a simple stick figure.

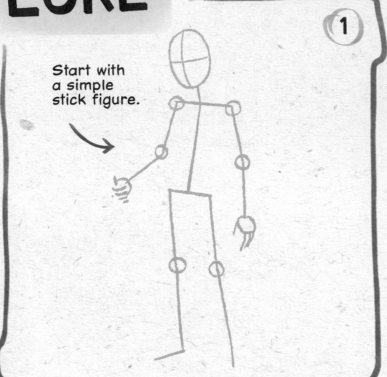

2

Add facial features.

Give Luke a helmet and start adding detail to his flightsuit.

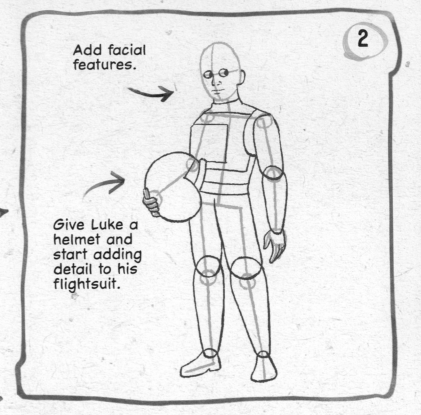

3

Add more details to his suit, including his breathing apparatus.

Add Luke's hair.

4

Add the final details and his rebel insignia.

Colour in Luke with the bright orange colours of the rebel fleet.

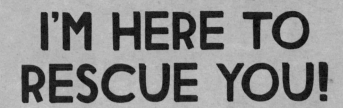

I'M HERE TO RESCUE YOU!

FINAL

FACT FILE

- SON OF ANAKIN SKYWALKER AND TWIN BROTHER OF PRINCESS LEIA

- BLOWS UP THE DEATH STAR AT THE BATTLE OF YAVIN

- LOSES HIS HAND IN A DUEL WITH DARTH VADER

X-WING

ONE OF THE REBEL ALLIANCE'S GREATEST STARFIGHTERS, THE X-WING IS SWIFT AND STEALTHY.

① Add four wings in flight formation as shown.

Draw a long pyramid shape for the nose and a long rectangle for the rear fuselage.

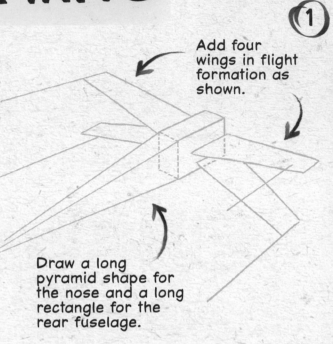

② Add laser cannons to the wings ready for battle.

Draw the engines and add details to the nose.

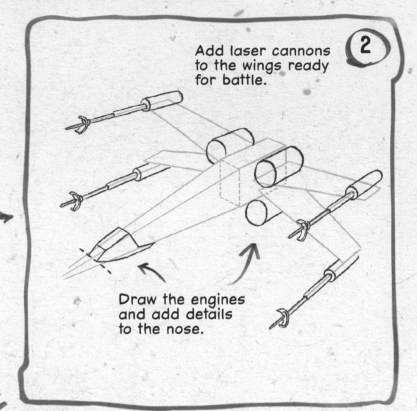

③ Add more details to the engines.

Add a cockpit window and an astromech droid for navigation.

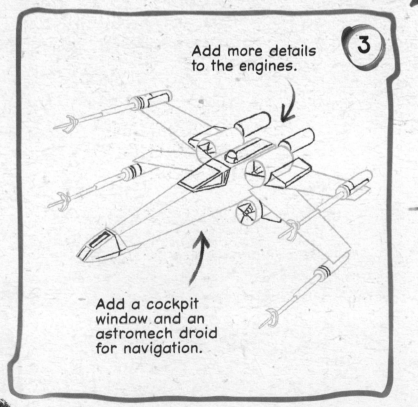

④ Add some final details to your starfighter.

Complete the X-wing with a red and yellow paint job.

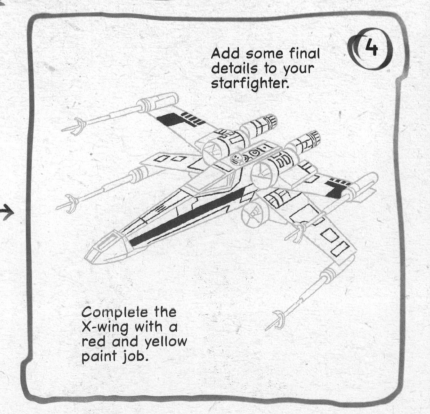

KYLO REN

THIS FORMER JEDI-IN-TRAINING IS STRONG WITH THE DARK SIDE OF THE FORCE. DO NOT MAKE HIM ANGRY!

1

Draw a stick figure outline of Kylo Ren and his lightsaber.

2

Add Kylo Ren's hood, belt and the front of his cloak.

Add long and short ovals for his legs, feet and arms.

3

Draw Kylo Ren's sinister mask.

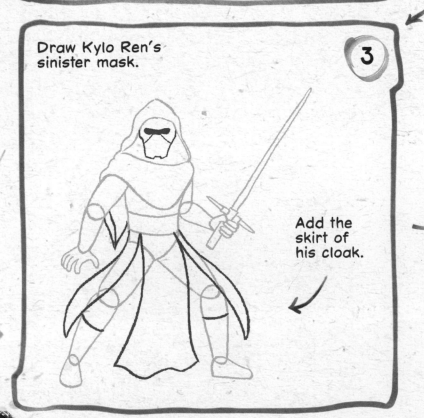

Add the skirt of his cloak.

4

Add the detail to Kylo Ren's outfit.

Add a glow to his lightsaber.

Rub out any pencil lines and colour in Kylo Ren.

I WILL FULFIL OUR DESTINY

FINAL

FACT FILE

- SON OF HAN SOLO AND LEIA ORGANA

- MEMBER OF THE KNIGHTS OF REN

- SEDUCED TO THE DARK SIDE BY SNOKE

- FEARLESS IN BATTLE

BB-8

1

Draw two circles for BB-8's head and body.

Rub out the overlapping lines.

2

Use the top circle to complete BB-8's dome head – don't forget his antennae!

Add in some detail to his body.

3

Add BB-8's photoreceptor.

Add the compartments on his body.

4

Add the final details to this lovable droid.

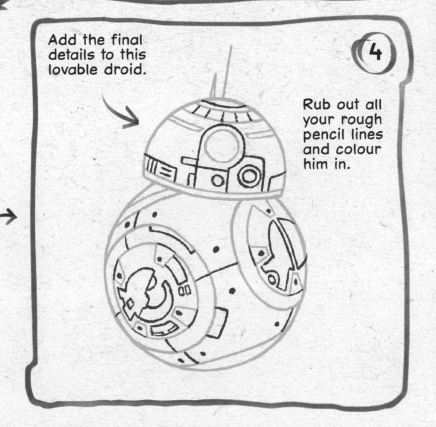

Rub out all your rough pencil lines and colour him in.

FINAL

BEEP BOOP BEEP

FACT FILE

- BB SERIES ASTROMECH DROID

- FOLLOWS HIS MASTER TO JOIN THE RESISTANCE

- EQUIPPED WITH A HOLOPROJECTOR, WELDING TORCH AND CABLE LAUNCHERS